Oakleaf Academy

First Day at Fairy School

Melody Lockhart and Roberta Tedeschi

This edition published in 2024 by Arcturus Publishing Limited
26/27 Bickels Yard, 151–153 Bermondsey Street,
London SE1 3HA

Author: Melody Lockhart
Illustrator: Roberta Tedeschi
Story Editor: Gemma Barder
Project Editors: Claire Baker and Joe Harris
Designer: Rosie Bellwood

CH010412NT
Supplier 10, Date 0924, PI 00009085

Printed in the UK

Chapter 1

Oakleaf Academy

Have you ever heard an owl sneeze? It sounds a little like this: "Atish-hoot!"

That's the first thing Poppy learned on her owl-bus journey to Oakleaf Academy. With every sneeze, Poppy flew into the air, then bumped back down on her seat.

The fairies and pixies around her—all dressed in the same stylish school uniform—didn't seem bothered by the bumps. They chattered away until the owl sniffled, then grabbed their seats.

"Atish-hoot-hoot-HOOT!"

This time, Poppy stayed sitting down, but her bag, a human coin purse, flew up. When it crashed back down on her head, the other students laughed noisily.

Poppy felt her face turn red. She looked down to hide it, as the owl-bus swooped closer to Oakleaf Academy. She spotted the school on top of a large tree stump, with steps leading up to a grand entrance. A spire stood tall next to a shiny glass dome. There was a garden, too, with a wishing well right in the middle of it. But what excited Poppy the most were all the smallfolk she could see.

As the owl-bus prepared to land, Poppy watched pixies, sprites, gnomes, and fairies mingling together, laden with bags and suitcases. Although she was a brownie, before today she had never met so many other folk like her in one place.

In fact, the only other smallfolk she had ever spent any time with at all were her father and occasionally her Aunt Hyacinth and Uncle Moss when they came to visit.

The owl-bus landed with a final lurch. Poppy clutched her bag tight as she spread her red, spotted wings. She didn't find it easy to flutter gracefully to the ground while holding a heavy bag, although she noticed that everyone else seemed to manage it perfectly well.

As another bird swooped down, the sudden gust of air from its wings caught

Poppy by surprise. The wind whipped under her wings and lifted her up off the ground, so that she tumbled back down, head over heels, in a kind of messy forward roll.

Poppy watched, slightly dazed, as the other bird—a sleek, chauffeur-driven swallow—touched down. A tall pixie with beautiful moth wings elegantly floated down from its back. The chauffeur followed, holding a set of perfectly matching luggage.

Poppy told herself to be brave. She was here to meet other smallfolk, after all. She'd agreed with her father that it was time to leave the library and learn all about the magical world she belonged to.

Standing up, Poppy called out, "Hello!" in her friendliest voice.

The pixie looked at Poppy, then down at her slightly battered bag, then back up at her face.

A moment's silence fell before Poppy spoke again. "I'm Poppy," she said. "I just arrived by owl-bus."

"How fascinating," replied the pixie, without smiling. "I *do* hope it wasn't the sneezing owl with the feather allergy. My name is Azalea."

Poppy tried to ignore the fact that Azalea didn't sound fascinated at all. "I've never been anywhere like this before.

In fact, I've never been anywhere except our library."

Azalea stared at Poppy as though she had started talking in ancient Trollish. "Whatever do you mean?"

"Oh, sorry," Poppy giggled. "The library is where my father and I live. It's part of this big old house, and it's crammed with enormous books."

"You mean to say that you live in a gallumpher's house?" Azalea said.

"Gallumpher?" asked Poppy. "Oh, no, I live in the library of a human house."

Azalea rolled her eyes. "Gallumphers *are* humans," she sighed, waving at the chauffeur to pick up her luggage. "At least, it's what most smallfolk call them. Most smallfolk except for you."

Poppy shuffled her feet uneasily. "Oh, I see," she said. "I suppose I still have a lot to learn about how things work. I've only really read about smallfolk in books."

Poppy's mind drifted back to the library again. Their cozy home, hidden behind the books on the highest shelf. The rocking chair her father had made, where he would sit each evening. Her bedroom decorated with bright postage stamps.

"What are you waiting for, Polly?" asked Azalea, following her chauffeur, who was hauling her entire set of matching luggage along the path to the school. "Where's the rest of your stuff?"

"It's *Poppy* actually, and this is it!" the brownie said brightly, picking up her bag and shaking off thoughts of home.

"That's all you brought?" asked Azalea. "You do travel light! Come this way—we need to go and register with Mr. Puck."

"Who's Mr. Puck?" asked Poppy,

trotting alongside Azalea and trying to keep up.

Azalea sighed. "Mr. Puck," she said, waving a hand in front of her, "is the teacher over there surrounded by new students. Gosh, you really do have a lot to learn."

Mr. Puck had a short beard flecked with silver and shiny goggles perched on his green top hat. As he chatted to the students, he bobbed up and down energetically, pointing with a long blue kingfisher feather quill that he clutched in one hand. "Oh, he's a leprechaun!" Poppy said, her eyes wide.

"Obviously," replied Azalea, with a slight snort.

In his other hand, Mr. Puck held a piece of leaf parchment. Poppy could see a sprite with bright red hair trying to read it over his shoulder. Her long limbs swooped this way and that, as her dragonfly wings buzzed and fluttered.

A pair of gnome twins stood nearby, the bright shells on their backs catching the sunlight. Poppy spotted a rainbow of pixies and even a few brownies standing around listening to Mr. Puck. When Poppy turned to talk to Azalea, she saw that she had already walked over to join the group.

"I just can't believe I'm actually here at Oakleaf!" Poppy said, hurrying to join her. Azalea shook her head slightly.

"Neither can I," muttered Azalea, and for a moment Poppy thought she looked nervous. Then the pixie added more loudly: "Now, if you don't mind, I'd like to listen to Mr. Puck's welcoming speech."

"Mr. Puck! Mr. Puck!" the red-haired sprite said. "Is it true that everyone gets cake on Fridays? I've heard that gallumphers eat fairy cakes, but do the cooks here make gallumpher cakes?"

Mr. Puck had just opened his mouth to answer, when the sprite spoke again. "Oh, Mr. Puck! When do we get to see our dorm rooms? My brothers told me that one room is full of seaweed from the bottom of the enchanted lake!"

The sprite giggled, and Poppy couldn't help joining in—until she saw Azalea's expression.

"Isn't she embarrassing?" Azalea said. "I pity her poor roommates—she never even pauses for breath!"

Mr. Puck cleared his throat loudly. Then he began talking in a firm but slightly flustered way:

"If you would all just settle near,
I'll tell you what you need to hear."

Chapter 2

A Lot to Learn

The crowd of smallfolk became quiet as Mr. Puck began his speech.

"Our newbies get a room to share,
You'll meet your roommates
once you're there."

Poppy's eyes widened. "Oh, yes," she whispered to herself. "Leprechauns always speak in rhyme!"

"Shhh!" said Azalea, as Mr. Puck continued speaking.

"When you've unpacked and settled in,
Your school enrollment will begin.
Ms. Peaseblossom, head of the school,
Will find a wand to be your tool.
The walled garden is where she'll wait,
So watch the clock, and don't be late!"

Poppy felt excited. She knew that she would get a wand at Oakleaf, but not on the very first day! Back home in the library, her father had made his own bookshelf for smallfolk-sized books. One of the oldest books on it was called *Wandology: A History of Wands.* There was one page of it that Poppy knew almost by heart, even though she'd never understood quite what it meant.

When a student is given their first wand, it does not yet have a spark at its tip. Only when a student discovers their true talent will the wand blossom with a gem-shaped spark for Groundling magic, a flower spark for Leafkin magic, a seashell for Fishscale magic, and a star for Ariel magic.

There were so many types of magic—but what did they all mean? The book had explained that with a little rhyme. Perhaps the author was a leprechaun, just like Mr. Puck!

If you love birds, bugs, and trees,
Leafkin charms will be a breeze.
If you dream of stars at night,
Ariel spells will fit just right.
If you dream of buried treasure,
Groundling spells will be a pleasure.
If you marvel at the ocean,
Fishscale magic's quite the notion.

Poppy sighed as she hugged her bag close, the copy of *Wandology* safe inside. She'd once seen her father's old wand in the back of a drawer, but he never used it, and she didn't think it looked particularly special.

Suddenly, Poppy felt a knot of worry in her tummy. What if being away from smallfolk for so long had somehow dulled his magic ... and hers, too? What if she didn't have a spark at all?

Mr. Puck's voice brought Poppy suddenly back to the present.

"All line up now, so you'll know,

Which room is yours and where to go."

When she reached the front of the line, Poppy told the leprechaun her name. He ran the tip of his quill along the leaf parchment until he found the right spot.

"Poppy dear, I do declare,

Your roommates are waiting there."

Poppy followed his pointing finger to where the red-haired sprite was fluttering excitedly next to Azalea.

Dropping his finger, Mr. Puck gestured to a plump little glowworm that had shuffled up beside his feet.

"Your new pet will light the way.

Take care of him night and day."

Then, Mr. Puck turned to the next student in line, and Poppy walked away.

"Hi, I'm Jessamy!" said the red-haired sprite, swooping over to give Poppy a hug. "We're going to be roommates! Isn't that fantastic? What's your name?"

"I'm—" replied Poppy. But before she could finish, Jessamy said, "Azalea's our roommate too! Are you a brownie? I LOVE brownies. I just love spotted wings!"

"Thank you, I—" started Poppy, but Jessamy was already on the move.

"Come on! Dazzle is showing us to our room! Do you mind if I call him Dazzle?"

Poppy couldn't help noticing that some of the smallfolk they passed stopped and stared at Azalea for a few moments before hurrying on. Jessamy fluttered over to her and whispered in Poppy's ear, "You're wondering what they're looking at, right? Well, Azalea is from a long line of important pixies. Her sisters were both top students at the Academy, so of course she's going to be someone special, too."

Jessamy didn't stop talking as Dazzle led them through the big wooden doors of Oakleaf Academy and up to the dormitory hallways. "My brothers told me that all newbies have a big sleepover in the first semester, but they could be lying, just like they were about the seaweed room, I guess. Then, of course, there are the Four Tests—I'm pretty sure they weren't lying about those. Then, after that, who knows what will happen because ..."

"The Four Tests?" Poppy interrupted.

Azalea, who had been walking slightly ahead, turned and sighed loudly. "Oh, please tell me you know what the Four Tests are?"

Poppy shook her head silently.

Azalea rolled her eyes. "The Four Tests are just the most important lessons you'll have this semester," she said. "They're used to find out what your spark will be."

"Wh–what exactly is a spark?" asked Poppy nervously. Azalea shook her head.

"You do have a lot to learn," she replied. "Your spark is the type of magic you have. A wand's spark is the symbol that appears at the tip of it. A jewel for Groundling magic, a flower for Leafkin, a shell for Fishscale, and a star for Ariel. All smallfolk have one of the four types." Azalea gave a little shudder. "Although why anyone would want to have Fishscale magic is beyond me."

"Then what are the tests?" asked Poppy. "What do we have to do?"

"They change every year," said Jessamy cheerfully. "To keep people from cheating

to get the spark they want."

Azalea snorted. "Your spark is who you are. You can't fake it. I know I'll be an Ariel, just like my mother and sisters."

At last, Dazzle stopped at a large wooden door, which Jessamy quickly flung open. Inside were two sets of wooden bunk beds, and on one of them sat a fairy with short, jet-black hair. "Well, you three took your time," she said.

Chapter 3

Wands

“I’m Ivy,” said the fairy. “Some snooty guy just dropped off all this luggage—I’m guessing it’s yours?” she added, with a nod of her spiky hair toward Azalea.

Azalea ignored Ivy and fluttered to the bunk bed on the opposite side of the room while Poppy told Ivy her name.

“Nice to meet you, Poppy. Hey! I see you’ve brought our room-pet. When I got here, all the glowworms were still asleep.”

“Isn’t he cute? I’m Jessamy. Shall we be bunk bed buddies? Great! I love the top bunk,” said Jessamy, as she fluttered to the bed above Ivy’s, leaving Poppy to share a bunk with Azalea. She smiled at Azalea as she picked up a sheet of leaf parchment from their bedside table.

"This tells us how to look after Dazzle," Poppy said. "I've never had a pet before."

"Just one of the many, many things you've never seen or done before," muttered Azalea.

"Hmmm," sighed Poppy, spotting the basket bed Dazzle was meant to sleep in.

"Well, that just means that every day will feel like a surprise party for you, Poppy!" said Jessamy with a smile.

Ivy frowned. "I'm not sure if that sounds like fun—or like it's terrifying!" she said, "And not much terrifies me!"

Poppy laughed. "Come on. We'd better get to the walled garden."

As Azalea fluttered off ahead, Poppy walked with Jessamy and Ivy. Ivy was unlike any fairy Poppy had seen. The ones she'd seen in books usually had long pink hair and bright dresses. But Ivy's hair was short and black, apart from a few pink streaks at the roots, and she wore big black boots with her uniform.

"I can't wait to get my wand!" said Jessamy, swooping between her two new friends. "I wonder what my spark will be. I wonder what your sparks will be! I wonder what we'll have for dinner ..."

"Do you think she ever stops talking?" Ivy whispered to Poppy with a laugh.

"She hasn't yet," Poppy replied. "But she seems really nice. I like her."

Ivy nodded. "Me too. I think the three of us could cook up a few adventures."

As Poppy stepped through the gates of the walled garden, she saw the most beautiful flower beds, each surrounded by a cobbled path that led to the middle of the garden. There, all the newbies were gathering around an older fairy with a kindly smile.

Ms. Peaseblossom, the principal of Oakleaf Academy, had faded pink hair with white streaks running through it. It was piled up on her head, with a pair of metal glasses perched on top. She was standing next to a flower that was as tall as she was. The flower had five petals, each a different shade to the next.

"Welcome, my needlessly nervous newbies!" said Ms. Peaseblossom. "Aren't you all just darling? I promise you're going to flourish here at the Academy. However, you can't begin until you have your wands!" Ms. Peaseblossom fluttered her wings lightly. "Jessamy, you're first!" she said. "Come over here, honey!"

For the first time that day, Poppy noticed Jessamy's cheery smile drop a little. "Now, pumpkin, there's no need to be nervous. Just place your hand

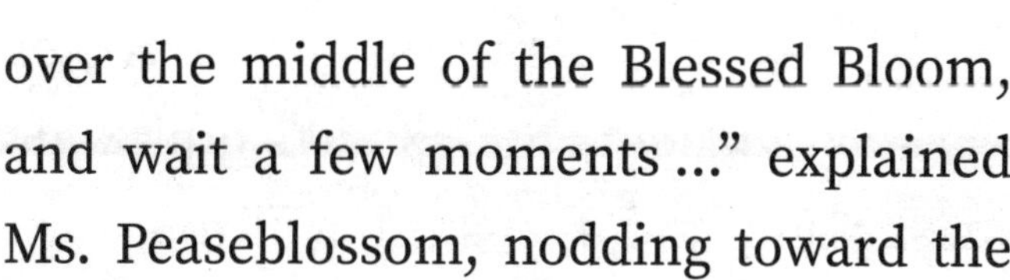

over the middle of the Blessed Bloom, and wait a few moments ..." explained Ms. Peaseblossom, nodding toward the tall flower beside her.

Jessamy slowly raised her hand. Poppy watched in amazement as a winding vine began to twirl and twist out of the Blessed Bloom. And at the end of it was a wand!

"What a fan-floral-tastic start, lovely Jessamy!" said Ms. Peaseblossom, as she snipped the wand free with a pair of tiny golden gardening scissors. "Now all you need to do is wait for it to gain its spark."

Next, it was Azalea's turn. She strode over to the Blessed Bloom and confidently placed her hand over it without even being told. Poppy wasn't surprised to see her wand shoot straight out of the flower.

Then, the gnome twins Poppy had spotted earlier took their turn together, and everyone gasped as two wands emerged from the flower at once.

Next was a grinning sprite who spoke to Ms. Peaseblossom using special hand movements. "Elderflower's deaf," said Ivy. "She's a sprite like Jessamy, and wicked smart." Then, it was Poppy's turn.

"Poppy dear, it's splendid to have you here at Oakleaf," said Ms. Peaseblossom kindly, as Poppy nervously stepped toward the Blessed Bloom. "Now, don't worry, sweetheart, you go ahead."

Poppy's hand trembled as she placed

it over the Blessed Bloom. With relief, she saw a stalk begin to grow. As it got longer, Poppy noticed that it was glowing with a warm red light. She glanced at Ms. Peaseblossom, who looked a little stunned. “Did I do it right, Ms. Peaseblossom?” Poppy asked, quietly.

Ms. Peaseblossom quickly returned to her usual smile. “Yes. Well done, my dear, blossoming brownie. Now, get going dear!”

Back in their room at bedtime, Poppy was checking the pet care sheet to find out how to tuck Dazzle up for the night. "What a day! I don't know how I'm going to sleep after all that excitement," she said to her roommates.

"Me neither!" said Jessamy. "Here's an idea—let's stay up all night finding out about each other instead. Then, we'll all be good friends!"

"Ugh!" Azalea held two soft pillows up to her ears. "If I have to start going to

school in the daytime, I'm going to need peace and quiet at night."

"Oh, yes!" Poppy said. "You're nocturnal, aren't you. I read about how pixies usually sleep all day in ..."

"... in your gallumpher library. We know!" Azalea interrupted grumpily, diving under the blanket.

"Come on, Azalea." said Ivy, "No one wants to be sleepy, but there are worse things in life. Did you hear what Olive and Oakley, the gnome twins, were saying?"

"Oooh, tell us, tell us!" said Jessamy.

"Last year, one of the newbies had to leave because they couldn't find their spark," said Ivy. "Their wand never blossomed. Just imagine!"

Poppy felt a knot form in her tummy again. This was *exactly* what she had been afraid of.

Chapter 4

The First Test

The next day, Poppy couldn't stop thinking about what Ivy had said. What if she'd lived away from smallfolk for too long, and she was the one with a wand that never blossomed?

Back in the walled garden, the newbies were listening to Mr. Puck, who was telling them about their classes. Each morning, they would study Spark Magic. Then, in the afternoon, they would learn about Smallfolk History, Creaturology, Enchanted Objects, and Gallumpher Avoidance (which everyone called Hide and Sneak).

"But what are we doing today, Mr. Puck?" asked Jessamy, excitedly.

"Now we start test number one,
I hope you find it lots of fun.
It shouldn't be too much to ask,
Down Oakleaf Mine you'll find your task."

"A mine?" Poppy whispered to Ivy, as all the newbies obediently followed Mr. Puck out of the garden.

"Yep, that's where all Groundling magic tests take place," Ivy said, and for the first time, Poppy noticed that her new friend's hands were shaking slightly.

Soon, they were standing in front of the opening of a tunnel littered with stones that led deep down into the dark ground.

"Groundling magic can be found,
By those who spend time underground.
They take their power from the jewels
As well as crystal—them's the rules!"

Mr. Puck proudly held up his own wand as he spoke, which displayed a shining green emerald at the tip.

"Follow now and don't be slow,
Who is a Groundling? Off you go!"

Jessamy, Olive, and Oakley were the first to speed down the tunnel after Mr. Puck, followed by a much slower Azalea, who stayed as far away from the muddy walls of the mine as she could. Ivy and Poppy smiled at each other encouragingly, then followed the others inside.

The walls were lit up with glowing jewels of every shade imaginable. The students followed Mr. Puck down twisting and branching tunnels until, finally, they came to a small opening. Mr. Puck spoke again, a mischievous smile on his face:

"Your task is this—don't mess around,
Just find your way back above ground."

Azalea rolled her eyes. "Is that all?

That's hardly going to be very challenging!"

Poppy took a deep breath. Surely she could remember the route back through the mine. Couldn't she? But Mr. Puck wasn't finished.

"The trouble is you'll have no light,

And have to use a different sight!"

With a click of his fingers, Mr. Puck made a small tunnel appear behind him. He stepped into it, then the tunnel closed up behind him. A moment later, the beautiful gems stopped glowing.

"What? No way!" cried Azalea. "He can't just leave us here in the dark!"

Poppy's heart began to thump when suddenly she felt a hand reaching out to grab her own. "Don't worry," said Ivy. "You probably know more than any of us with everything you've read."

In the darkness, Poppy could hear the giggles and footsteps of other students.

"We'll give you a hint!" cried a voice that Poppy recognized as Olive's, one of the gnome twins. "Use a different sense!" called Oakley. With that, their footsteps disappeared into the distance. "Let's stick together," said Jessamy, in a much quieter voice than usual.

"No thanks," said Azalea. "I'm sure I can figure out a boring Groundling task on my own."

"Good luck, then, Miss Clever-Wings," snorted Ivy, as Azalea hurried off.

"The twins talked about using another sense," whispered Ivy to Poppy and Jessamy. "But it's not like we can taste or sniff our way out of here, can we?"

"Hmm," said Poppy, thinking hard. "I did read in one of my dad's books that you can feel the magic in jewels by touching them—and touch is a sense, isn't it?"

"Ooh, yes!" said Jessamy, "And when I touched a crystal near the entrance, it felt warm, a little bit like a magical glow."

Ivy touched the wall closest to her. "Hmm, the crystals here feel super-cold."

"That's it!" cried Poppy, "There's a huma ... uh ... gallumpher game I've read about where they find things by calling 'hot' when they're close to it and 'cold' when they're farther away. Could

the jewels' magic tell us the same thing?"

"What, so warmer jewels would take us closer to the exit, and colder ones would lead us farther away?" asked Jessamy.

"It's worth a try," said Ivy. "Come on!"

The friends crept through the dark tunnels, carefully running their fingertips along the walls. Whenever they touched a jewel that was icy cold, they would change direction again, feeling for warmer jewels as they went.

Finally, Poppy found herself blinking in the bright sunshine as she stepped out of the mine. "We did it!" she said, her voice a little squeaky with surprise.

"It would have been a hundred times harder without you!" said Ivy, smiling.

"That was fun!" said Jessamy. "Who knew books could be so useful? The only books my brothers ever brought home had titles like *Space Gallumpher Squad*!"

A little way ahead, a small crowd had gathered around Olive and Oakley. As the

friends got closer, they saw that the twins' wands had blossomed, with a twinkling diamond floating at the tip of Oakley's wand and a sapphire at the tip of Olive's. Beside them, Mr. Puck bobbed excitedly from one shiny green boot to the other.

"The first ones to come from the dark,
You have now found your Groundling spark!"

"Ugh!" Everyone turned to see who was the last one to come out of the mine. "Just look at my uniform!" huffed Azalea.

Her face was red with fury as she brushed mud from her skirt. Ivy giggled and Jessamy tried hard not to join in.

"Don't you worry if you're sticky,
Groundling magic is quite tricky," said Mr. Puck with a smile. But Azalea's face didn't look as though that made her feel any better.

Chapter 5

The Second Test

Poppy was surprised to see Oakley and Olive ready to take on the second test a few days later. All the newbies were waiting in the woodland next to the Academy, wearing their sports uniforms and waiting for a pixie teacher named Ms. Pine.

"What are you two doing here?" Poppy asked the twins. "I thought you'd both found your sparks."

"We have!" said Oakley, proudly holding up his wand. "But smallfolk need to know about all kinds of magic, not just their own, so each student must do every test."

Olive nodded. "That's not all," she said. "Apparently, your spark can change—if you're *even better* at another task than the one that gave you your spark."

"Pfft," Oakley scoffed. "That's nonsense. Anyway, I love my spark and I'm keeping it forever."

"It is not nonsense!" cried Olive. "I heard it from a girl who heard it from someone two years older than us, so there!"

"Attention, Oakleaf newbies!" called Ms. Pine, stopping Olive and Oakley's squabbling. Poppy turned to see a tall

pixie with a long ponytail waving her wand in the air to gather everyone around.

"Today's a big day—your Leafkin test. I hope you're all feeling limber!" Ms. Pine's green eyes sparkled in the sunlight.

"Limber?" whispered Jessamy. "What on Earth's that?"

"Ready for exercise," sighed Azalea.

"Now, students, each of you must race around the woodland collecting as many silver acorn cups as you can," said Ms. Pine. "There are many of them hidden in and around the trees. We'll be using them as bowls and cups in the school cafeteria this year."

Ms. Pine raised her flower-tipped wand as a signal, and a small flock of red-breasted robins swooped down to the woodland floor. "Mount your birds, please, quick smart!"

“H–hello,” Poppy said, approaching one of the birds. The robin chirruped happily and lowered its wing for Poppy to climb aboard.

“I want to see nice, smooth gliding from you all. It’s not a race—this time! We’re looking for a strong bond between you and your companion,” Ms. Pine said. Then, she blew into her whistle to signal the start of the test.

Poppy watched as Azalea and Jessamy took flight without any hesitation. She held on to her own bird's saddle as all the other students took off one by one. How was she going to get off the ground? "Um, little bird could you …" Poppy began. "If you don't mind, I mean, could you fly for me?"

With a gentle flutter of its wings, the robin took off, following the rest of the flock. Poppy felt the wind rush through her hair as she gripped the saddle tightly. She had no idea how she was going to stay upright and collect acorn cups at the same time.

"Use one hand!" called Ivy, as Poppy reached the treetops.

"Whoa! This is fun!" shrieked Jessamy, swooping through the branches, her arms already full of cups. "Wahoo!"

Poppy nervously took one hand off the robin's saddle. To her amazement, she didn't immediately fall off! She looked in all the trees and steered her robin toward the branches of a particularly wide one, when she saw a glint of silver between its leaves. The robin slowed for a moment as Poppy took a deep breath, reached out her free hand, and scooped two acorn cups into her bag. "I did it!"

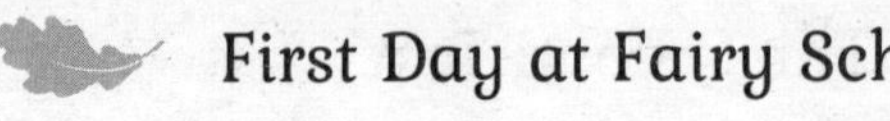

"I think I'm getting the hang of this!" Poppy called to Ivy as they flew past each other.

"Animals aren't really my thing," Ivy called back. "But I do like this little red-breasted dude. A few black feathers in his wings, and we could really become friends!"

Poppy laughed as she swooped to grab another acorn cup. At that moment, two brown and red streaks whooshed past them. “Who were they?” asked Poppy, gripping on to her saddle.

“Jessamy and Azalea!” called Ivy. “They’ve been leading the way ever since the beginning of the test. I think Azalea wants to prove herself after her calamity in the mines.”

Poppy gazed upward as Azalea and Jessamy skillfully soared on their birds. Azalea’s face was set in sheer determination, and Jessamy’s was filled with a huge grin.

“Come on!” said Ivy. “Let’s not worry about them. After all, we have our own test to tackle.”

“I’m going to start searching on the forest floor,” Poppy called back. Then, she carefully guided her robin down through the trees until it landed on the ground with a gentle bump.

"Thank you so much!" she said, stroking the bird's soft head feathers as she jumped down. "I'll take it from here."

Poppy searched under rocks, between bushes, and behind mushrooms. When she saw Ms. Pine looking at a stopwatch, she grew concerned that she was running out of time. Then, she heard a worried cry.

"Help!"

But who was it and where could it be coming from?

"Help! I'm stuck!" the voice said again. Poppy cupped her ear, then fluttered toward the sound to find Oakley completely tangled in some twisting vines at the base of a great oak tree. "What happened?" Poppy asked, rushing over. "Are you hurt?"

"I'm fine," huffed Oakley. "Apart from only collecting three acorn cups, falling off my robin, and getting all tangled up."

"Oh dear, where's Olive?" Poppy asked.

Oakley pointed to the sky. "Up there. She doesn't know I fell off. Promise me you won't tell her, please!" he said.

"I promise," Poppy giggled, as she freed Oakley from the tangled vines.

"Thanks so much," said Oakley, as he got up at last. "But what about your test?"

"I think I can spare a few minutes to help out a friend," said Poppy with a grin.

Together, Oakley and Poppy dashed back to the starting line.

"C'mon, you two!" called Ms. Pine, clicking her stopwatch. "Now line up everyone, bags in front of you."

Ms. Pine walked briskly along the line of students. When Poppy emptied her bag, eight acorn cups tumbled out. "Not too bad," said Ms. Pine. "But you started off pretty well up there. What happened?"

Oakley's face burned red with shame. "Oh, I ..." Poppy started. "... I sort of tumbled off my robin."

"Hmmm," said Ms. Pine suspiciously, looking from Oakley to Poppy, just as Jessamy joined the line. Beside her was a fluffy-tailed squirrel with very fat cheeks.

"And who is this fellow?" said Ms. Pine.

"I hope it's okay," said Jessamy. "Only my bag was really full, and this little guy said he could help me out."

Then, Jessamy tipped out her bulging bag as the squirrel emptied his cheeks. "Splendid work! Twenty-five cups and some truly wonderful smallfolk and animal cooperation," said Ms. Pine.

Just then, Jessamy's wand began to glow. "Well, if I'm not mistaken," said Ms. Pine, "that might suggest Leafkin … oh!"

As Jessamy held up her wand, there was a burst of light. Her new spark looked like a delicate dandelion seed head.

Chapter 6

The Sleepover

Poppy couldn't believe how fast her first week at Oakleaf Academy had gone!

"Come on!" said Ivy, leading her toward the newbies' hall. "It's the traditional Oakleaf Newbies First Semester Sleepover. I've got some really good scary bedtime stories to tell everyone!"

Arriving at the hall, Poppy saw a cozy fireplace. In front of it, students were curled up on squishy beanbags, perched on mushroom-shaped stools, or kneeling on cushions. Jessamy and Elderflower were handing out acorn cups full of sweet-scented apple nectar.

"Where's Azalea?" Poppy asked.

"She said she hates sleepovers, so she's

not coming," Ivy replied. "Her loss!"

Poppy looked around the room, where pixies, sprites, gnomes, and brownies were all having fun together. She just knew Azalea should be here, too, so she hurried back to the dorm room.

"Please come!" said Poppy, spotting Azalea crouched next to Dazzle's basket.

"Thanks, but no thanks," replied Azalea. She quickly closed the large textbook she was holding, which Poppy noticed was named *The Art of Flight*.

"But there's spiced apple nectar," said Poppy. "And Elderflower is setting up a game. It'll be so much fun!"

"I'm not here for fun," snapped Azalea. "I'm here to study—and to find my Ariel spark, of course."

Poppy frowned. "Even I know that school isn't all about studying," she said. "What about making friends?"

Azalea rolled her eyes.

"I know," said Poppy, staring at Azalea's pile of homework. "What if I promise to help you with your History of Smallfolk essay? I got the best grades for mine."

Azalea slowly closed her textbook. "Okay, fine," she sighed. "But I absolutely will not be sleeping on the floor."

Back in the hall, Poppy and Azalea found all the newbies sitting in a circle in front of the fire. In the middle was a nutshell filled with leaves.

"The game is called Trick or Tale! I love it, it's so much fun!" said Jessamy, as everyone shuffled to make space in the circle for Poppy and Azalea. "On each of these leaves is a word. All you have to do is pick out a leaf, read the word, then either perform a trick or tell us a tale!" Then, she picked up the bowl and held it toward Ivy.

"My leaf says 'Makeover,'" said Ivy. "Well, that's an easy one ..." She grinned as she pulled a small black hairbrush out of her sleepover bag and handed it to Jessamy. "It's not your usual fairy

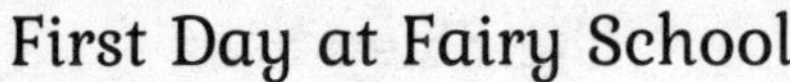

hairbrush, but try it," she said.

Jessamy pulled the brush through her curls. The room gasped as they watched her bright red hair turn jet black. "Wow!" said Jessamy, giggling. "I could get used to this!"

"Sorry, it won't last long," said Ivy. "You have to use it every day to get hair as cool as mine! Your turn, Jessamy."

Jessamy rummaged in the bowl before pulling out her own leaf. "My word's

'Surprise.'" In a flash, she swooped out of the room and returned a moment later holding an umbrella. "Well, that's hardly very surprising," Azalea whispered to Poppy, though not all that quietly.

"Don't you have to wait for the surprise, Azalea?" said Ivy.

"Oh, yes," said Poppy. "Look!"

As Jessamy flew to the top of the room and opened the umbrella, silver sparkles began to rain onto all the newbies. But as soon as the glitter landed on them, it disappeared completely. "A little something my oldest brother created," Jessamy said. "He enchanted the umbrella using his Ariel magic. Sometimes, he can be the most annoying brother ever, but I have to admit he is pretty smart."

"Your brother is an Ariel," said Azalea, her voice squeaky with shock.

Jessamy nodded and grinned. "Top of his class. Don't you dare tell him, but I'm proud of him. Okay, your turn next!" she said, passing the bowl to Poppy.

Poppy's stomach did a somersault. She'd been having so much fun watching her friends perform tricks that she hadn't even thought about having to do one herself. The only enchanted thing she owned was a bookmark her father had given her, which could find any word in any book as quick as lightning. Her hand shook a little as she pulled out a leaf.

"'Home,'" Poppy read out, breathing a sigh of relief. "I suppose I'll tell you a tale, then."

Poppy took a deep breath. She knew her home was probably quite different to that of most of the other students, but she was proud of it anyway.

"My home is in a library of a hu … I mean, a gallumpher's house," she began. "It's just me and my dad. We have lots of books, and we love to read together by the fire. He knows a lot about smallfolk, so even though I'd never met a sprite or a pixie until this week, I feel like I know you all already!"

Poppy smiled as Ivy put a friendly arm around her shoulder. She glanced at

Azalea and, to her surprise, saw a small smile creep across her face.

"It's probably nothing like your home," Poppy giggled. "I bet you have more than two bedrooms, to start with!"

"Um, 17, to be exact," said Azalea.

Ivy snorted and passed the bowl to Elderflower, who picked out the word "Fright."

Elderflower described the time when she came face to face with a gallumpher's big tabby cat outdoors. Every so often, she used sign language, too, and Poppy noticed that the sign for cat looked just like whiskers. "When he opened his mouth, I thought he was going to gobble me up," said Elderflower with a shudder, "but it turned out he was just yawning. He soon curled up and went to sleep so I flew away right over his head!" Her bright laugh filled the hall.

Next, Oakley picked out the word "Confusing." He nodded at Olive mischievously, and together they scuttled off into a corner. A moment later, the twins reappeared wearing little hats to cover their hair. In their matching nightwear, it was almost impossible to tell them apart.

"Oakley!" called Elderflower, pointing at the twin on the right.

"No way!" giggled Ivy. "That must be Olive, for sure?"

The room cheered as the twins took off their hats to reveal who was who.

"Trick or tale! Trick or tale!" sang Jessamy, as she fluttered over to Azalea with the bowl. Right away, Poppy noticed Azalea's smile fall.

The fire crackled as Azalea slowly picked out a leaf. "'Family,'" Azalea read aloud. She stood up and smoothed her white silk pajamas. "Most of you already know my family," she said proudly. "We descend from a long line of important

pixies. My grandparents, parents, and both my older sisters are Ariels. Not just Ariels, of course, but some of the best, most talented Ariels ever seen. And I intend to follow in their footsteps."

Azalea sat down again, looking very pleased with herself. As the next student chose their leaf, Poppy whispered, "How nice to have such a famous family."

Azalea shrugged. "Hmm, I guess. Just so long as you're every bit as perfect as everyone else in it," she said.

Poppy moved closer. "Nobody's perfect, you know. And I don't see why you should be either," she said.

Azalea stood up suddenly and glared at Poppy. "How would *you* know?" she huffed. And then, with a noisy whip of her wings, she swept out of the hall and back to the dorm.

Chapter 7

The Third Test

A few days later, just before their Enchanted Objects class started, Azalea was proudly showing the other students her new sparkling star-shaped ring.

"It's from my mother," said Azalea. "She says it will match the Ariel spark on my wand once I get it."

"It's lovely, Azalea," Poppy said. She felt a bit sad that they hadn't talked much since the sleepover and was glad when Azalea thanked her with a smile.

Just then, Ms. Glimmer, a brownie with short hair, a big smile, and dangly leaf earrings, arrived. "Sorry I'm late," she said. "I have some exciting news! Your Fishscale test will be next Monday. Gather by the wishing well at 9 a.m. sharp. Mr. Pondweed doesn't like latecomers!"

Azalea gazed at her ring. "I should go, really," she whispered to Poppy. "Though there's not much point, for me at least."

"It's exciting!" Poppy replied. "I wonder what it's like to have a Fishscale spark?"

"I imagine you smell like fish and grow scales or something ..." said Azalea, her wings shuddering at the thought.

"I'm surprised you showed up," Ivy said, as Azalea met her, Poppy, and Jessamy at the wishing well the following Monday.

"Why wouldn't I? A good student needs to know about all types of magic," replied Azalea. "Even if it is Fishscale."

"Oh, yes!" said Jessamy. "I mean I love my Leafkin spark, but I can't wait to do this test. I've heard all kinds of stories about Mr. Pondweed from my brothers. Apparently he used to fight pirates and has a chest full of treasure!"

"Really?" said Ivy. "Are you sure your brothers aren't pulling your leg? And where is he, anyway? There's nothing here to tell us what to do but … oh, look!" Ivy peered inside the well's bucket. Inside, she could see a leaf rolled up into a scroll and a pile of glittering gold coins.

"Oooh!" said Jessamy, reading from the leaf scroll. "'To find out if a Fishscale spark's for you, throw a coin into the well.' Oh, I see, it's a kind of wishing well. That must be part of the test then."

"Well, I *wish* it wasn't!" sighed Azalea. "But I'm not hanging around here, let's get started!" she said, neatly flipping a coin into the well. Then, a moment later, she disappeared, leaving a gold shimmer where she once stood.

Next, Poppy picked up a coin. But where would she end up? Swallowing hard, she flipped the coin into the well and blinked. When she opened her eyes, she was standing next to Azalea beside an underground lake in a dark cave. The faraway voices of her fellow newbies, who had yet to flip the coin, echoed around the walls of the underground chamber. In the middle of the lake, a smallfolk-sized ship with tattered sails bobbed up and down.

“Students!” echoed a loud voice. As Jessamy and Ivy, leading Elderflower by the hand, appeared beside Poppy and Azalea, they all turned to see where it was coming from.

“Now that ye all be here, we can begin!” the voice boomed. Finally, they spotted a gnome on the other side of the lake.

He wore a striped T-shirt, a blue coat, and had a white beard. In one hand, he held his wand, which had a beautiful seashell at the tip. But his other hand wasn't there at all. It was just a hook. "My name be Mr. Pondweed. Whatever ye've heard about me be likely true—so listen well!"

Jessamy and Poppy both grinned. For once, Jessamy's brothers were right!

"The Fishscale spark be one of the finest sparks—some say best of all," Mr. Pondweed said. "So ye've got to earn it!"

"For this task, ye'll be workin' in pairs," Mr. Pondweed said. He raised his wand into the air and swirled it once. Before they knew it, the students were standing together in twos. Poppy was with Elderflower, Jessamy with Olive, and Ivy had been paired with Azalea, though neither of them looked happy about it. Next, maps magically appeared, one to share between each pair.

"All that ye need to be doin' is to follow the map to find me treasure!" said Mr. Pondweed, before he jumped back onto the pirate ship and disappeared. A shocked silence fell over the lake.

"I knew it!" trilled Jessamy. "I knew he'd be a pirate!"

"He's not a pirate," said Azalea, the map gripped in her hand. "He's just a gnome who talks strangely. Right, let's get to it."

"This is not going to go well," Ivy huffed.

"Good luck!" Poppy called, as her friends began to flutter off in different directions around the huge lake. Poppy felt for her wand, which was tucked safely in her belt. Maybe today would be the day she found her spark.

Elderflower unfurled the map and pointed toward a narrow path at the edge of the lake. "Let's go!" said Poppy. Elderflower held the map up, glancing at it now and then. It didn't make much sense to Poppy, but Elderflower strode on confidently with Poppy following behind. She seemed to know which way to go just by looking at the patterns of slimy seaweed on the wall or the way the few rays of sunlight that leaked through the cave walls hit the water.

After a few twists and turns, they arrived in a smaller cave. Its walls were dripping with water. To their surprise, Ivy and Azalea were already there.

"Are you sure this is the place?" Ivy asked, looking around.

"It's perfectly simple," Azalea huffed. "Anyone with a tiny sprinkle of magic could read that map."

Poppy's cheeks burned red. If she

couldn't read the map, perhaps she didn't have magic after all.

"Thank goodness you two are here!" Ivy said, fluttering over to Poppy and Elderflower.

"Yes, another pixie to help will make this easier. After all, we're fast learners!" said Azalea, signing her words to Elderflower at the same time. "It took me no time at all to learn sign language from one of my cousins, and now I'm practically fluent."

Elderflower smiled. "Almost!" she said kindly, "But look, 'cousin' looks like this. Otherwise, it's 'grasshopper.' You're doing so well, though, keep it up!"

Elderflower showed them an "X" on the map. "There's a clue here," she said. "Something must be hidden in this cave."

"So, where should we start looking?" asked Poppy. Ivy was already busy peering into cracks and running her hands along the walls.

"Honestly, you two, it's like you just crawled out of a mouse hole!" Azalea huffed, and Poppy felt her cheeks redden again. "Stand back, this is how smallfolk should look for magical items." Azalea took a deep breath and closed her eyes. Then, she raised one hand and began to wave it slowly around.

Suddenly, Elderflower began to flutter

excitedly. From the back of the cave, a small shell was floating toward them. Poppy's eyes widened as the shell moved even closer and landed softly in Azalea's hand.

For a moment, Azalea stared at the shell. Then, she flipped it open and showed them the small silver key inside it. "You see," she said, her voice wobbling a little. "Easy."

"Even I have to admit that was impressive!" said Ivy, grinning at Azalea. "But where do we go now?"

Elderflower fluttered to the edge of the cave and looked toward the lake. "I can see a line of coral in the water, and it's leading right to the pirate ship!" she said.

Full of excitement, they all flew across the water to the ship. Mr. Pondweed was standing on the deck by a large wooden chest with a rusty metal lock on it. "Congratulations, me hearties!" he said, stroking his beard with his one good hand. "Ye've found me treasure, but can ye open it?"

Azalea hesitated slightly before she put the silver key into the lock and slowly turned it. As it clicked open, the glow of gold and the sparkle of jewels spread over all the other students who had now joined them on the ship.

"Good for you!" Poppy said, clapping. But Azalea wasn't smiling. She was staring at Elderflower's wand. It had started to shimmer with blue sparkles as a shiny shell appeared at the tip.

"Oh, no …" said Azalea, staring at her own wand, which had started to shimmer, too. "No, no, NO!" she cried, just as it sparked and an even shinier shell shone at its tip as well.

Chapter 8

The Final Test

Poppy had never seen Azalea in such a bad mood. All Azalea did was go to lessons, do her homework, then go to bed. But a few times, Poppy had woken in the night to see her roommate pacing up and down, glaring at her wand furiously.

"Try not to worry about Azalea," Ivy urged Poppy, as they walked to the

observatory for a lesson on Ariel magic. "She'll have to learn to live with her Fishscale spark. She was obviously given it for a reason. Elderflower loves hers."

"It's not just Azalea," said Poppy quietly. "I haven't even found my spark yet. What if the stories are true and I'm one of the smallfolk who never finds their spark?"

"I haven't found my spark yet either," Ivy said, as they walked into the observatory. "But don't worry, it just takes some smallfolk longer than others."

Poppy's eyes widened as she took in the huge circular hall of the observatory, with its glass domed roof and rows of wooden benches around the edges.

"Good day, my dear newbies!" said Ms. Peaseblossom, as the students gathered around her. "Now, let's get started."

"Today's lesson will help you prepare for your Ariel test next week," said Ms. Peaseblossom with an encouraging smile. She took out her wand and Poppy noticed the glittering silver star at its tip. As Ms. Peaseblossom gracefully waved it, the glass dome turned an inky blue, filled with glittering stars and planets. Everyone gasped in wonder.

"Which one of my superb students can tell me the importance of stardust?" said Ms. Peaseblossom.

Jessamy's hand shot into the air. "Stardust is used for all kinds of magical things!" she said excitedly. "Spells, tricks, cooking ... we even use it to help the crops grow on the farm where I live."

"Wonderful!" said Ms. Peaseblossom, clapping. "Collecting stardust is one of the most important jobs smallfolk with

Ariel sparks can do. But it's also very dangerous, since stardust can only be collected at great heights, which are difficult to reach. And so our test will take place here in the observatory, where you can each try collecting it safely."

A ripple of excited chatter bubbled through the students.

"Settle down, my little blossoms!" said the principal. "I have one more

announcement. I've invited your families to watch this special final test."

Poppy's heart soared. She'd missed her father so much and couldn't wait to see him again.

"I'm looking forward to seeing everyone's folks!" said Jessamy. "Does anyone else in your family have black hair, Ivy?"

"Absolutely not!" giggled Ivy.

"It will be nice to see your parents and sisters, won't it?" Poppy said to Azalea.

Azalea shook her head. "I don't want them to come," she said, miserably. "I haven't told them about my stupid Fishscale spark yet. They're going to be so disappointed!"

As Ivy peeked through the curtains, Poppy, Jessamy, and Azalea could hear the low murmur of parents chatting as they took their seats on the benches.

"What can you see?" whispered Jessamy.

"Smallfolk who look a little bit like us but with more wrinkles!" replied Ivy.

Jessamy and Poppy laughed, but Azalea remained silent. "Your family will still be proud of you," Poppy said gently. "You're probably the smartest girl in the whole class, whatever spark you have."

Azalea shrugged. "That just shows me how much you still have to learn," she said coldly.

"Come on, girls!" trilled Ms. Peaseblossom. "Time to take your seats!"

As the newbies filled the rest of the benches, Poppy nervously looked along the benches full of visitors. She spotted a family of stylishly dressed pixies who she thought must be Azalea's family, but where was her own dad?

"Welcome!" said Ms. Peaseblossom, fluttering high beneath the observatory dome. "Parents, family, former students, welcome! Today is the final test of the first semester and our students will be catching stardust under our dome. The school rules say that newbies are not allowed to fly high enough to catch stardust from the sky, so today we have our own jars of it, specially caught for this test."

With that, Ms. Peaseblossom gave a little clap, and Mr. Puck, Ms. Pine, Mr. Pondweed, and Ms. Glimmer walked in carrying large jars of what looked like sparkly gold and silver glitter. With another little clap, each teacher unscrewed their jar, and the glitter flew into the air, swooping this way and that.

"Wow! Stardust!" Ivy whispered to Poppy, her eyes wide.

The stardust twirled about in sparkling ribbons, leaving trails of glitter across the domed roof.

"Come, come!" said Ms. Peaseblossom, as she ushered the students off their benches, and Ms. Pine handed them each a net made out of fine, silky spiderweb. She gave the non-flying students a swig of floating potion, too. As they lined up, Poppy glanced at Azalea. She looked more determined than Poppy had ever seen her.

"Ready to flourish, my fabulous newbies?" Ms. Peaseblossom said. "Let's get to work!"

Poppy pushed herself into the air and spread her spotted wings. Clutching her net tight, she soon found a trail of stardust to chase. As Ivy passed her, she saw that her friend already had a few glints of

stardust in her net. Nearby, Jessamy was giggling with Elderflower, both of them having more fun flying around than actually catching anything!

Suddenly, a gust of wind sent Poppy into a spiral and nearly knocked her net out of her hand. Azalea! Poppy watched as she whizzed by, swinging her net and gathering stardust as fast as she could.

"Azalea!" Poppy called. "Slow down! You're going to hurt your wings!"

"Or knock someone else's wings off!" said Ivy, hovering just above Poppy.

"I don't care!" cried Azalea, her eyes flitting about as she looked for more stardust. "I heard what Olive said before the Leafkin test. If smallfolk do better at another test, their spark can change. I'm going to prove my spark is Ariel, not stupid, stinky Fishscale!" Then, she zoomed past Poppy and Ivy, her net held out ready to catch more stardust.

"She can't really believe that!" said Ivy. "I'm sure it's never happened before!"

"I think she'd try anything to change her spark," Poppy replied.

Ivy sighed. "Oh, well, she'll just have to find out herself. Come on, we've got a test to do!"

As Ivy dashed off, Poppy looked first at her empty net, then around the observatory. There! Some stardust! Poppy swooped to catch it when, down below, she spotted her aunt and uncle cheering her on. Her heart soared for a moment, then sank again. Her father wasn't with them.

Then, before the students knew it, Ms. Pine had blown her whistle to signal the end of the test.

All the newbies lined up in front of Ms. Peaseblossom, panting as they clutched their spiderweb nets.

Poppy emptied out what little stardust she had managed to catch. "Never mind, dear," said Ms. Peaseblossom. "It's a very tricky test." Poppy sighed. It would take a miracle for her wand to blossom with an Ariel spark after that performance.

"My, my, Azalea! Most impressive!" Ms. Peaseblossom nodded at Azalea's huge pile of stardust. Azalea looked at her family in the crowd, keeping her wand hidden behind her back.

"Goodness me, young Ivy!" continued Ms. Peaseblossom. "I haven't seen such a fabulous stack of stardust in all my years at Oakleaf!"

With dismay, Azalea turned back to see that Ivy's pile was twice as large as hers. Poppy grinned at Ivy, who had turned as pink as the roots of her hair. Suddenly, Ivy's wand started to glow. As she stared at it with wide eyes, golden sparks began to fizz from the tip as a glittering star blossomed. "Oh, Ivy!" said Ms. Peaseblossom with delight. "You're blessed with the Ariel spark!"

Azalea slowly brought her own wand out from behind her back. She stared hard at it, willing it to change. But the pretty seashell stubbornly remained.

Azalea swept past Poppy and out of the observatory. Poppy was sure she'd seen tears in Azalea's eyes, but as she began to follow her, she heard a familiar voice.

"Oh, Poppy dear, well done!" Poppy stopped to hug her Aunt Hyacinth.

"Thank you," said Poppy, although she knew she hadn't done that well at all. "Where's Dad? Did he come?"

Aunt Hyacinth glanced at Poppy's Uncle Moss beside her. "He hasn't been very well, Poppy. And he couldn't quite face the bumpy owl-bus ride," said Uncle Moss. "I think he's got a point. We ended up on that dreadful one with the feather allergy, sneezing all the way!"

Poppy tried to not to look too disappointed. Besides, she had other things to worry about. She'd just finished her final test, and her wand still hadn't blossomed. Why had everyone else found their spark but her?

All she could see around her were students excitedly showing their wands to their families. Poppy felt tears prick her eyes, even though Aunt Hyacinth tried to be kind about her dull wand.

"I'm sure your spark will appear soon, dear," she said, seeing Poppy's sad face.

But it was worse than that. Not only did she have no spark, but she had no dad to show it to, either.

Chapter 9

The Midnight Feast

"We have to do something! It's our last week of the semester!" Jessamy insisted, as she twirled around the room she shared with Poppy, Ivy, and Azalea.

"I can't believe it's the end of the semester already," said Poppy, stroking Dazzle's back as he drifted off to sleep

on the rug. "It feels like we've only just arrived!"

Poppy looked around the room. Her bag was almost packed and she was looking forward to seeing her dad again. She glanced down at her wand, lying by her side. The only thing that would have made her first semester perfect would have been to find her spark.

Azalea was sitting on her bunk, her matching luggage not even half-packed. She hadn't said a word to Ivy since the last test. Ivy knew it wasn't her fault that her wand had blossomed with the Ariel spark, but she still felt bad for Azalea.

"I wish there was something we could do to cheer her up," Ivy whispered to Poppy. "Even I feel sorry for her!"

Poppy smiled. "Here's an idea. When children visited the gallumpher's house, they used to have secret parties at night. They had snacks and drinks and lots of fun. I think they called them midnight feasts," said Poppy.

"A MIDNIGHT FEAST!" cried Jessamy, landing on the rug next to Poppy and Ivy. "That's the best idea I've EVER heard! I love having a clever friend who's always full of good ideas!"

Poppy picked up her wand. "It's just a shame there isn't a Bookworm spark for knowing stuff or a Light Bulb spark for good ideas," Poppy said, sadly. "Or my wand might have blossomed in the first week here."

"Hey! I could make a batch of my famous sprite cupcakes," Jessamy said, putting her arm around Poppy, who was nodding enthusiastically. "They always cheer people up—even my grumpy oldest brother, when he broke his wing and couldn't fly for a whole month!"

"What about you, Azalea?" Ivy asked.

"It might be fun?" Poppy added.

Azalea shrugged, hugging her pillow.

"Azalea, you HAVE to come!" Jessamy said, fluttering over to Azalea's bunk. "It won't be the same without all four of us. Please, please, pleeeeeeeease!"

Azalea stood up and pushed her hair off her face. “Oh, okay!” she said. “If you could just stop talking for five minutes, I’ll do whatever you say!”

Together, the four friends tiptoed out of their room, down the dimly-lit hallways and into the school kitchen. The kitchen smelled of that evening’s very-berry pie, with a touch of spicy cinnamon still in the air. Every shelf was crammed with jars and pots and pans.

“Right, Ivy, find a cupcake tray. Poppy, see if you can turn on the oven,” Jessamy said, as she searched the shelves. “All I need is flour, rosewater, honey, and a tiny sprinkle of ... oh ...”

“What’s the matter?” asked Azalea.

“I need a sprinkle of stardust for the cupcakes, it’s my special ingredient” replied Jessamy. “But the jar’s empty.

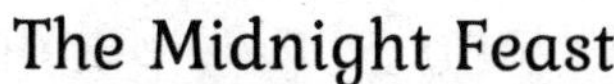

They must have used it all for the test."

"Never mind, we can always just ..." Poppy began, just as Azalea flew swiftly from the room. Poppy, Ivy, and Jessamy hurried after Azalea, as she whooshed into the Academy gardens. "What are you doing?" asked Ivy, once they finally

caught up with her.

"Going to gather stardust, of course!" replied Azalea. "If I manage to collect it for real, from real stars, my wand will have to change!"

"Azalea! You can't!" Ivy said. "I don't much like rules, but that's a school rule even I wouldn't break!"

"That's easy for you to say, you have your Ariel spark," Azalea snapped. "And now I'm going to get mine!" With that, she pushed off the ground and zoomed high into the night sky.

"Ooh, she's going to get into trouble!" said Jessamy, hopping from one leg to the other. "Us newbies aren't allowed to fly higher than the observatory roof!" But Azalea kept flying higher. "What are we going to do?"

"We'll have to go after her," said Ivy. "And bring her back before anyone notices she's gone!"

The three friends pushed off the ground, shivering as the cold night air wrapped around them. "Azalea!" Poppy cried. "Azalea! COME BACK!"

Soon, all four friends were higher than they'd ever flown before. The Academy looked tiny beneath them, and the air was getting colder and colder. But Azalea kept flying higher until they could hardly see her at all. Poppy noticed that Jessamy was trembling with cold, and she decided what to do. "Go back down, Jessamy!" she called. "If anyone catches us up here, they might take away our wands."

"What about you?" Ivy asked, huddling close to Jessamy to keep her warm.

"I haven't got my spark—and I don't know if I ever will," Poppy replied. "It won't matter if I lose my wand!"

Ivy frowned, but before she could say another word, Poppy put on a burst of speed, soaring even higher. Her wings felt tired and sore, but she knew she had to keep going. She searched the dark night sky. At first, there was nothing but inky blackness and a few twinkling stars, then she spotted Azalea hovering just ahead of her. She was shivering with cold, and her wings had started to droop. "Azalea!" Poppy cried. "STOP!"

With one last push, Poppy flew through the sky to Azalea, just as Azalea's wings stopped fluttering at all and she began to fall downward.

"It's okay, Azalea!" said Poppy, swooping to catch Azalea under her arms and beating her wings as hard as she could. "I've got you!"

Jessamy and Ivy watched on nervously from a path in the gardens of the Academy as Poppy carefully guided Azalea down to the ground. They rushed over just in time to help, them both make a soft, safe landing and finally, all four friends were safe.

Shivering and exhausted, Azalea blinked and looked at the faces around her. She stared at Poppy, who was panting with exhaustion beside her. "Wh … why did you do that?" Azalea asked. "You would have been in so much trouble if a teacher had seen you."

Poppy sat up slowly. "Because I'm your friend," Poppy said. "We all are."

Azalea looked from Poppy to Jessamy and finally to Ivy. "I guess it's true," Ivy said. "And we couldn't let you get expelled. Oakleaf wouldn't be the same without our little Princess."

Azalea managed a small smile. "Thank you," she said. "I've been so silly …"

"This is all very wonderful!" said Jessamy cheerfully, despite her shivers. "But could we talk about this back in our room? Sprites aren't built for the cold, you know. I'm freeeeeeezing!"

The four friends laughed as they slowly got to their feet. They were just walking back to their room when Poppy suddenly stopped. "What's the matter?" asked Ivy, as Poppy took her wand from her pajama pocket and held it up.

It was glowing with a warm red light.

"What is it? What's happening?" asked Jessamy, excitedly.

"Her wand ..." said Azalea. "It looks like it's going to ..."

Suddenly, the air was filled with a light so bright that the four friends had to shield their eyes for a moment. As the brightness faded, Poppy was stunned to see that her wand had finally blossomed. But it wasn't a jewel, or a dandelion, or a seashell, or even a star at the end of her wand. It was a glowing red heart.

"What is it?" asked Jessamy, her eyes wide with wonder.

"Well, that's something I've never seen before," said Ivy.

"It's so beautiful," said Azalea.

"I don't understand," said Poppy, staring at her wand in disbelief. "What does it mean?"

Chapter 10

A Spark For Poppy

Poppy, Ivy, Jessamy, and Azalea waited nervously outside Ms. Peaseblossom's office. They knew the only way they would be able to find out about Poppy's spark was to tell Ms. Peaseblossom everything that had happened in the Academy gardens the night before.

"Please do come in!" called Ms. Peaseblossom in a welcoming voice. The friends pushed the door open and stepped into Ms. Peaseblossom's warm, snug office. Poppy noticed the neat fire in the small fireplace and rows of shelves stacked with leaf scrolls. In the middle, Ms. Peaseblossom sat behind a desk carved from an old oak branch.

She pushed her glasses on top of her head and smiled at her visitors. “Well now, what can I do for you four lovelies?” she asked, kindly.

The friends looked at each other for a moment, before Poppy pulled out her wand. The warm light from the heart tip cast a red glow over Ms. Peaseblossom’s astonished face. “Goodness gracious!”

she cried. "I think you'd better explain how this happened."

Azalea stepped forward right away. "It's my fault, Ms. Peaseblossom," she said bravely. "I wanted to change my spark, so I did something silly. I flew high above the Academy—much higher than I know we're allowed to fly."

Ms. Peaseblossom raised her pink eyebrows as Azalea continued. "Then I started to get tired and my wings began to droop. If Poppy hadn't been there to save me, I don't know what I would have done."

"And once Poppy did save her, that happened," said Ivy, pointing to Poppy's wand. "It just kind of exploded with light and then the heart appeared."

Ms. Peaseblossom fluttered out from behind her desk toward Poppy. "Is this true?" she asked. Poppy nodded silently. "Hmmm, I wasn't certain, but I could see from the day your wand sprouted out of the Blessed Bloom that there was something different about you, Poppy."

Then, Ms. Peaseblossom fluttered to one of her highest shelves.

"But what does it mean?" asked Jessamy "Is Poppy a super-brownie? Can she turn invisible? Is she going to grow to the size of a gallumpher?"

Ms. Peaseblossom took an old, dusty scroll from a high shelf and chuckled. "Not quite," she said, fluttering to the ground and unfurling the scroll. On it was a drawing of a Heart spark and some tiny writing that began: "All about the Very Rare Heart Spark."

"Well, fancy that, you've been given the Heart spark," Ms. Peaseblossom said. "It's so rare, we don't even test for it at

Oakleaf. In fact, I've only ever known one other smallfolk in my life who had it."

Poppy blinked in amazement. "But … what does it mean?" she asked.

"It means you must have a very big heart," Ms. Peaseblossom said, "and I can well believe it. Not many smallfolk students would take time out of their own test to help out a naughty gnome …"

Poppy gasped. "How did you know about that?"

"Or let their partner work everything out in another test to let them shine," Ms. Peaseblossom continued. "Or save their roommate from a terrible accident. Not much gets past me, my dear. You showed great kindness to Oakley, Elderflower, and Azalea—and your spark is your reward."

"So, what can it do?" asked Azalea. "What special powers does Poppy have?"

"The Heart charm is the most powerful spark of all," read Ms. Peaseblossom from the scroll. "It is a great gift, though hard to control. It contains elements of all four of the main sparks: Leafkin, Groundling, Fishscale, and Ariel."

"We knew you could do it!" said Jessamy, giving Poppy a hug.

"You couldn't be this nice for nothing!" added Ivy, joining Poppy and Jessamy.

"Delighted as I am for you, Poppy," continued Ms. Peaseblossom as she rolled up the scroll, "I do need to address what went on last night. And how you broke school rules on flight height, Azalea."

The four friends all looked down. "Perhaps a short essay on the benefits of school rules is in order. Hand it in next semester." Ms. Peaseblossom smiled as Ivy groaned quietly. "Now shoo! Pack your things, and have a great break!"

Ivy, Jessamy, and Azalea quickly fluttered out of the office, but Poppy lingered in the doorway. "But Ms. Peaseblossom," she said, "I'm still not sure why the Heart spark chose me."

Ms. Peaseblossom smiled kindly. "Don't worry, you will in time."

"What a semester!" Jessamy said, fluttering around the room, collecting odd socks and hair ties and popping them in her suitcase. "I feel like we've been at Oakleaf Academy forever!"

Azalea was silently packing everything into her matching luggage set and wouldn't look at anyone.

"I could never have imagined everything that's happened," said Poppy. "I feel like I've been living inside one of my dad's books since I got here!"

Ivy fluttered close to Poppy. "Looks like someone is feeling a little jealous of your spark," she said quietly, looking over toward Azalea.

Poppy frowned. She thought she and Azalea had become friends, but now she wasn't sure. "Azalea," she said, heading over to their shared bunk bed. "Is everything all right?"

"Not really," Azalea replied, placing a neatly folded pair of silk pajamas into her bag. "I feel dreadful."

"Well, you shouldn't!" said Ivy, crossly. "You should be happy for Poppy—she deserves her spark."

"That's not what I mean," replied Azalea, finally turning away from her packing. "I feel dreadful for how I've behaved toward you all."

"I thought I was only at Oakleaf to be the best and get my wand to blossom with the Ariel spark," Azalea continued. "I thought that was more important than having fun and making friends. But Poppy's made lots of friends and had lots of fun—and she's been rewarded with the rarest, most powerful spark of all!"

Poppy blushed. She still couldn't quite believe it herself.

"And now I know that there are more important things than being the best at everything," Azalea said. "Things like having really good friends."

Azalea put her arms around her friends as Dazzle shuffled to join in. "I realize I was so lucky to be put in a room with Poppy, and you, Jessamy—even though you never stop talking—and you, Ivy. You never let me get away with anything!"

Ivy giggled. "Actually, I think you're pretty cool," she said. "And I absolutely LOVE your luggage set!"

Azalea took a deep breath. "Now I know I can face my family and tell them about my Fishscale spark," she said. "Who knows? If anyone can make slimy seaweed and scaly fish cool, it's going to be me!"

Poppy's bag sat at her feet as she waited for the owl-bus to take her home again. She crossed her fingers, hoping it wouldn't be the owl with the feather allergy again.

Gripping her wand, she felt the warmth of its glow in her hand. She still wasn't sure how to use its powers, but she was determined to learn and do her best.

Just then, Poppy felt her hair ruffle as Azalea's sleek, chauffeur-driven swallow swooped down next to her. She looked around for Azalea, but to her amazement, she saw her father climb down from the back of the swallow, waving his thanks to the chauffeur.

"Dad!" Poppy shouted, dropping her bag and running toward him. "What are you doing here? And arriving by chauffeur-driven swallow, too!"

Poppy's father hugged her tightly. "Nothing to do with me," he said. "Somebody I think you know sent a message to say her swallow would pick me up this morning and bring me here."

"Azalea! Was it you?" Poppy asked, as Azalea crept out from behind a bush.

"Well, I couldn't let my best friend and her dad catch a sneezing owl-bus home now, could I?" Azalea said. "You go first, and the swallow will come back for me."

Poppy giggled as her father helped her lift her bag onto the swallow's back. Then, they both climbed on board, and Poppy snuggled up as they flew away. The school looked smaller and smaller below them. Poppy was excited at the thought of being back in the library again, but she knew she'd miss her new friends—and she couldn't wait for all the adventures they would share at Oakleaf Academy next semester.